Weird New World

"Land the ship," ordered Blork.

"Aye-aye, Captain," said Moomie Peevik.

Suddenly they heard the screech of tearing metal. The ship began to rock back and forth.

"We're gonna die," moaned Appus Meko. "I knew it. We're gonna—"

CRASH! BLAM!

The door fell open. The crew tumbled out.

They fell through the air, then landed on some soft, squishy plants.

"Cool!" said Blork. "It's like big pillows! We can—"

He was cut off by a thundering roar of anger. Looking up, he said in a very tiny voice, "Uh-oh!"

The giant creature looking down at them began to lick its lips.

Books by Bruce Coville

The A.I. Gang Trilogy:
Operation Sherlock
Robot Trouble
Forever Begins Tomorrow

Bruce Coville's Alien Adventures:
Aliens Ate My Homework
I Left My Sneakers in Dimension X
The Search for Snout

Camp Haunted Hills:
How I Survived My Summer Vacation
Some of My Best Friends Are Monsters
The Dinosaur That Followed Me Home

Magic Shop Books:
Jennifer Murdley's Toad
Jeremy Thatcher, Dragon Hatcher
The Monster's Ring

My Teacher Books:
My Teacher Is an Alien
My Teacher Fried My Brains
My Teacher Glows in the Dark
My Teacher Flunked the Planet

Space Brat Books:
Space Brat
Space Brat 2: Blork's Evil Twin
Space Brat 3: The Wrath of Squat
Space Brat 4: Planet of the Dips
Space Brat 5: The Saber-toothed Poodnoobie

The Dragonslayers
Goblins in the Castle
Monster of the Year
The World's Worst Fairy Godmother

Available from MINSTREL Books

BRUCE COVILLE

SPACE BRAT 5: THE SABER-TOOTHED POODNOOBIE

Illustrated by
Katherine Coville

A MINSTREL®
BOOK

Published by POCKET BOOKS
New York   London   Toronto   Sydney   Tokyo   Singapore

for each other

This book is a work of fiction. Names, characters, places and incidents are products of the author's imagination or are used fictitiously. Any resemblance to actual events or locales or persons, living or dead, is entirely coincidental.

A MINSTREL PAPERBACK *Original*

 A Minstrel Book published by
POCKET BOOKS, a division of Simon & Schuster Inc.
1230 Avenue of the Americas, New York, NY 10020

ISBN: 0-671-00870-6

First Minstrel Books paperback printing October 1997

10 9 8 7 6 5 4 3 2 1

A MINSTREL BOOK and colophon are registered trademarks
of Simon & Schuster Inc.

Printed in the U.S.A.

Contents

HOMEWARD BOUNCED

The rocket ship tossed and turned. It lurched and twisted. It bent sideways and went *sproing-g-g-g-g!*

It was stuck in the Transcendental Whoopee Warp, and it couldn't get out.

Inside the ship Blork and his crew were having the same problem. They tossed and turned. They lurched and twisted. They bent sideways and went *sproing-g-g-g-g!*

It was not a pretty sight.

In the center of the ship, Dr. Pimento was holding two loose wires together. The wires were snapping and sparking.

Dr. Pimento was snapping and sparking, too. He was surrounded by a blue glow, and bursts of light were coming out of his ears. He was jumping up and down, shouting "Wha-hooo-hooo-hooie!"

Though this was not a pretty sight, either, it was fairly interesting.

"Pull the wires apart!" shouted Blork.

At least, that was what he *tried* to shout. What actually came out of his mouth was a sound like the death warble of a Friskan P-tooie bird.

That was one of the problems with being in the Whoopee Warp. You were never sure how your words were going to come out. It could be funny, but Blork wasn't laughing. He was terrified. If he couldn't get Dr.

Pimento to take the wires apart, they would be stuck in the Whoopee Warp forever!

He decided to try a flying tackle.

Unfortunately, the ship's floor was coated with poodnoobie slobber. (Another problem with the Whoopee Warp was that it made Blork's pet poodnoobie, Lunk, drool even more than usual.) Blork made it halfway across the cabin. Then he slipped in the slobber, slid sideways, and slammed into a seat.

He thought about having a tantrum. But he didn't have time for that kind of nonsense.

He began crawling across the floor.

The ship made a particularly big *sproing-g-g-g-g,* and things got weirder than ever. Dr. Pimento turned purple. Little balls of yellow light swirled through the air. The slobber on the floor turned sticky. Suddenly Blork felt as if he were crawling through a glue spill.

Moomie Peevik was clinging to her chair and trying to keep her bows from eating her head. "Skippy!" she shouted. "Do something!" To her surprise, the words came out normal. (In the Whoopee Warp, *anything* was possible—even normalness!)

Skippy the Dip was using his propeller hat to stay hovering in midair, which seemed the safest place right now. Flying to Dr. Pimento, he shouted, "Let go, you super doofus!"

"I can't!" cried Dr. Pimento, who was vibrating like a Bonzergonian humming beetle.

Skippy dipped down and slapped the scientist's hands apart.

The connection was broken. Instantly the ship popped out of the Whoopee Warp and back into time and space as we know it.

Dr. Pimento blinked and took a deep breath. "Wow!" he said. "That was really cool. Wanna do it again?"

"GET ME OUTTA HERE!" cried a desperate voice.

4

It was Appus Meko. He was locked in the little room where Skippy had once hidden to stow away on the ship. The reason he was there was that the crew was trying to get back to the planet Splat, and Dr. Pimento had a theory that the Whoopee Warp would *sproing* the ship back to the home of whoever was locked in that closet.

Appus Meko was supposed to be alone in the closet, but Blabber the Fuzzygrumper had gotten locked inside, too.

"Ow!" cried Appus Meko now. "Stop biting me!"

"Oh, good," said Moomie Peevik, sounding relieved. "Blabber must be all right."

Blork pulled the door open.

Appus Meko staggered out. "Am I dead yet?" he groaned.

Blabber came running out after him. "Luddle-luddle-luddle!" he cried, skittling across the floor and throwing himself into Moomie Peevik's arms.

"You're not dead,"

said Skippy. "Just whiny and obnoxious. But you've always been that way."

Appus Meko scowled. "Who let that fuzzy-grumper in with me?"

"No one *let* him in," said Blork. "It just happened."

"Well, where did we just happen to end up?" asked Appus Meko. "Are we home or not?"

"We're home," said Moomie Peevik, who was operating the control panel. "At least, I think we are." She frowned. "There's something weird going on. I'm sure that's Splat right below us. But somehow it looks . . . different."

"Take the ship down so we can get a closer look," said Blork, remembering that he was captain.

Moomie Peevik pushed some buttons on the control panel.

The ship swooped closer to the planet. Blork scowled. The planet below them looked *almost* like Splat.

Almost, but not quite.

Appus Meko grabbed his elbow. "Don't you recognize that?" he whispered in horror.

"Recognize what?" asked Blork.

"Those continents. Those oceans. That's Splat all right. But it's the way Splat looked *a hundred million years ago!*"

Blork gulped. Appus Meko was right. Their teacher, Modra Ploogsik, had showed them pictures of the way scientists thought Splat used to look. Pictures that looked *exactly* like the planet below them.

"How can that be?" asked Moomie Peevik. Her voice was small and frightened.

"Ooh! Ooh! I think I've got it!" cried Dr. Pimento, who was working something out on his fingers. "When Blabber went into the closet with Appus Meko, it threw us off course. Not off course in space. Off course in *time!* The Whoopee Warp brought us home all right. But it also brought us back to Blabber's primitive roots."

"Why would it do a thing like that?" asked Blork.

Dr. Pimento thought for a moment, which made his eyes go around in circles. Then he snapped his fingers. "Your people didn't evolve on Splat. They came by rocket, right?"

Blork nodded.

Dr. Pimento was very excited. "Oh, this is beautiful! It's so profound. It's so strange! I love it!"

"Love what, you big silly stick?" shouted Skippy.

"The combination of Appus Meko and Blabber confused the Whoopee Warp, especially since Appus Meko is, in some ways, a newcomer to Splat. Oh, strange and wondrous is the Whoopee Warp. I have to make some notes on this."

He whipped out his pocket computer and started to scribble on it with his fingertip.

As he did, the ship lurched and made a screaming sound.

"Captain Blork, Captain Blork!" shouted Moomie Peevik. "We've got big trouble."

"What is it?" cried Blork.

"The trip through the Whoopee Warp messed up the engines again. I'm losing control. We'd better land and make repairs."

"Down there?" cried Appus Meko. "You've got to be kidding! We'll all die!"

"We could stay here and die," muttered Dr. Pimento, who wasn't really paying attention to the conversation.

"Land the ship," ordered Blork.

"Aye-aye, Captain," said Moomie Peevik. She began pushing buttons. She wrinkled her brow and stuck the tip of her tongue between her teeth. She concentrated so hard that her nose holes were no bigger than pinpoints.

Suddenly they heard the screech of tearing metal.

"What's going on?" cried Blork as the ship began to rock back and forth.

"It's an earthquake!" cried Dr. Pimento. "How interesting!"

"We're gonna die," moaned Appus Meko. "I knew it. We're gonna"— CRASH! BLAM!—"die. . . ."

The door fell open.

The crew tumbled out. They fell through the air, then landed on some soft, squishy plants.

"Cool!" said Blork as the plant stems bent sideways. "It's like big pillows! We can—"

He was cut off by a thundering roar of anger.

Looking up, he said in a very tiny voice, "Uh-oh . . ."

The giant creature looking down at them began to lick its lips.

2

SHIP, WRECKED

The monster had a huge mouth, five horns, and yellow eyes the size of the ship's windows. Its tail thrashed and whipped behind it. The thick blue tongue thwocking in and out over its fangs was longer than Dr. Pimento was tall.

"What a fascinating creature," muttered Dr. Pimento, scribbling a note to himself.

"It's a fremmis!" whispered Moomie Peevik in awe. The six-thousand-pound fremmis was the ugliest creature on the planet Splat. A prehistoric fremmis was worse than anything she had ever imagined.

"And the ship is caught on its horns!" cried Skippy.

"Ai-yi-yi, we're gonna die-die-die!" cried Appus Meko.

"Don't let it see you're afraid!" ordered Blork.

"Duh!" said Skippy. "I think it already knows that!"

The fremmis reached forward. The crew turned to run—except for Skippy, who was too round for running. He revved his propeller and shot high into the air.

The fremmis roared in frustration. Which way should it grab? It looked from side to side, grunting and snorting. Then it started toward Blork and Lunk—probably because they were close together, which meant more meat in one place.

Lunk stopped, frozen in terror, staring at the monster.

"Come on, boy!" cried Blork desperately, tugging at Lunk and trying to get him to move.

The scaly claws of the fremmis closed around them.

It raised them toward its face.

"Let go of my friends, you great lumbering clot!" shouted Skippy. He was floating above the monster, but suddenly came crashing down onto its head. He flew up and dropped down over and over again—*Thwack! Thwack! Thwack!*

The monster's eyes crossed. It dropped Blork and Lunk. With a wild roar it stretched up toward Skippy.

Crash! Bang! Clunk! The ship fell off the fremmis's back.

Skippy soared out of reach.

The fremmis turned back toward Blork and Lunk.

"Yeee-hah!" cried Skippy. Hurtling toward the monster one more time, he smacked it solidly on the skull, then bounced away.

Bellowing with anger, the fremmis leaped high into the air. It snatched at the chubby Dip, but he floated just above its grasping claws. The monster crashed to the ground, landing with a thud that shook the spaceship.

"Yeow!" it cried, lifting each of its feet in turn, as if they had been burnt. It stared at the travelers, hissing angrily. Then it turned and scurried into the forest, which was made of tall leafy things that were sort of like trees, but not quite.

"Heh, heh, heh," said Skippy as he floated to the ground.

"You saved us!" cried Blork.

Skippy looked embarrassed. Then he said, "Well, you saved me from having to stay with those Dips back on my home planet. So let's call it even."

"We're all gonna die," moaned Appus Meko.

"Shut up," replied everyone.

"Let's go exploring!" said Dr. Pimento.

"Shouldn't we do something about the ship first?" asked Moomie Peevik.

Dr. Pimento sighed. "I suppose so."

Glancing around nervously for any sign of dangerous creatures, the little group went back to the ship, which was lying on its side.

"It doesn't look too good," said Blork.

"I wonder if the poor thing can still fly," said Moomie Peevik, gazing at it sadly.

"Well, there's only one way to find out," said Blork.

They climbed inside, which wasn't easy.

The ship wouldn't even start.

"We're stranded in the past!" screeched Appus Meko.

"Are you practicing to be a reporter or something?" asked Skippy.

"Let's see if we can figure out what's wrong with it," said Blork.

Moomie Peevik and Dr. Pimento started taking things apart, looking for the damage. After a few minutes Dr. Pimento got side-tracked and started looking for new ways to put the pieces back together.

"Look!" he cried. "If you connect these three parts like this, you can make an atomic antenna squiggler."

"Give me those!" cried Blork, snatching the pieces away from him.

"Don't you like it?" asked Dr. Pimento. He sounded surprised, and a little hurt.

"It's wonderful," said Moomie Peevik kindly. "But right now we have to see what we can do about fixing the ship."

Dr. Pimento rolled his eyes. "Oh, I already figured that out. Didn't I tell you? We can't fix the ship without making some new parts. It's going to take at least three weeks. And I don't think it will work anyway."

"You mean we really are stranded here?" asked Blork, trying to remind himself that he was the captain, and captains aren't supposed to panic.

"Probably. Can I have those pieces back now?"

"No! Come on, we have to think. Let's get everyone together."

When the little group had gathered back in the control room, Blork explained the situation.

"*The Conquering Female Warrior Scouts Survival Guide* says the first things you need to worry about are food, water, and shelter," said Moomie Peevik.

"We can use the ship for shelter," said Blork.

"And I've already checked out the food situation," said Skippy, patting his stomach and burping. "We've got enough to last about three days. The ship could make more if we could get it started, but since we can't power it up, the food-i-lators won't work."

Blork sighed. "Then the first thing we'd better do is go exploring. We'll have to find food if we're going to live through this."

"We're more apt to *be* food," said Appus Meko.

"Now there's an idea!" said Skippy. "If we use you for bait, maybe we can catch something big enough to feed us for a month or two. Of course, we'd have to find some animal that likes a little whine with its dinner."

Appus Meko scowled at him.

"Come on," said Moomie Peevik. "If we're going on an expedition, we should see what we can find in the ship's supplies."

"Good idea," said Blork.

Their ship had been owned by Blork's arch-enemy Squat, who gave it to Blork after Blork defeated him on the Planet of Cranky People. The crew had been so busy since they got the ship they had not really had a chance to check out what was on board. Or even to name it, for that matter.

They headed for the lower levels.

"Zappo guns!" said Skippy happily, after a few minutes of digging around in the store-room. "These should be useful."

"Here's some helmets!" called Moomie Peevik, from the other side of the room.

"Look, some fribbulating ecto-transwhams!" cried Dr. Pimento, rubbing his hands with delight.

"What good are those?" asked Skippy.

"I dunno. I just think they're cool."

Skippy sighed and went back to examining the piles of stuff.

"Oh, wow!" cried Appus Meko. "A personal force-field generator." He put on a weird-looking hat and flipped the switch on its top. "Look, I'm invincible!"

"I can still see you," said Blork.

"Not invisible," said Appus Meko. *"Invincible!"*

"Could be," said Skippy. "But you're still obnoxious."

Appus Meko glared at him.

Soon the group was ready. Blork, Dr. Pimento, and Moomie Peevik were wearing helmets. So was Blabber, since Moomie Peevik had found a tiny helmet that would fit him just right. Skippy kept his flying beanie, of course. Appus Meko wore the force-field hat.

Blork led the way, with Lunk beside him. Skippy floated along in the rear position because he could spin around easily to see if anything was following them.

Leaving the ship, they started into the forest.

It was deep, and dark, and strange. Weird noises echoed among the plants. Insects with eyes like fist-sized jewels and wings as wide as Dr. Pimento was tall flitted among the trees. Shafts of green light filtered through the feathery leaves.

They heard a whooshing noise as something went swinging past them.

"What's that?" asked Skippy.

"Good grief!" whispered Moomie Peevik, her voice filled with awe. "It's a giant seers."

"A what?" asked Skippy.

"They get around by swinging from tree to tree by their ears," said Blork. "But that one's ears must be twenty—no, *thirty!*—feet long."

"Better watch out," said Appus Meko. "When you see a seers, there's bound to be a grobutt nearby."

"Shhhh!" hissed Moomie Peevik. "I think I hear it!"

The ground shook. A mighty THUD! THUD! THUD! filled the air.

"That's a grobutt all right," said Blork.

A moment later they came out of the forest and into a clear area. They blinked in the sunlight.

"Good grief!" cried Appus Meko. "Look!"

3

SABER-TOOTH, VEXED

Thundering toward them was an animal that looked a lot like Lunk. It was different in three ways:

1. Its fur was long and shaggy (though still purple),

2. It had two fangs the size of swords,
                    and

3. It was so big it made Lunk—who was pretty big himself—seem like a baby.

"Run!" cried Moomie Peevik.

"We're all gonna die!" screamed Appus Meko, diving under a huge green leaf.

"Come on, boy," said Blork, tugging at Lunk. "We've got to get out of here."

But Lunk wouldn't move. He stood staring at the prehistoric version of himself in fascination.

"Come *on!*" cried Blork urgently.

Lunk planted his feet, solid and stubborn, and refused to budge. Blork looked at the horrible creature racing toward them. Fear shot through his body. He wanted to run. But he couldn't abandon Lunk.

"Take out your Zappo guns!" he cried.

The saber-toothed poodnoobie began to slow down as it got closer to them. It was starting to look more curious than angry.

"Hold your fire," said Blork.

Trotting up to them, the saber-tooth began to sniff at Lunk, who trembled, but didn't move away.

The saber-tooth made a questioning noise. Then it bent and picked Lunk up in its giant mouth!

"Hey!" cried Blork. "You put him down!"

The giant creature looked at Blork as if he were some kind of funny little bug. Then it turned and started to trot away, still holding Lunk in its mouth.

"Fire!" cried Blork.

Five Zappo guns blasted out at once. Their green rays splattered across the poodnoobie's giant purple butt.

The creature froze in place.

Blork hurried forward. Lunk, still dangling from the saber-tooth's mouth, squirmed and whined.

"We'll get you down, boy," said Blork, though he had no idea how they would do that. "Come on, everybody—help me!"

He grabbed a fistful of the giant poodnoobie's fur and began to climb its leg. The fur was thick and shaggy. The leg was like a small tree. The climbing was easy, and before long Blork had reached the creature's shoulder. He was just trying to figure out what to do when the Zappo ray wore off.

"Uh-oh," said Blork in a small voice.

The saber-tooth gave a mighty shake, as if

it was trying to get rid of some annoying bug. Blork sank his hands into its fur and held on for all he was worth.

The creature began to run.

"Wait!" Blork heard his friends cry. *"Come back!"*

He also heard the sizzle of Zappo rays. This time they didn't affect the giant poodnoobie at all. It ran faster and faster, its six mighty legs pumping as it crashed through the ferns and giant mushrooms.

Suddenly they came to the edge of a swamp. Blork knew that in his own time poodnoobies lived in swamps. He wondered if it was the same back in this time. Next he wondered what the creature was going to do with Lunk. Then he wondered what prehistoric poodnoobies ate—and if one might stretch its diet to include a young Splatoonian like himself.

The poodnoobie hurried through the swamp. Sometimes it ran on solid paths. Sometimes it splashed through the green, slimy water. At last it came to an island that had a high, rocky center. Following a well-worn path, the saber-tooth made its way up the rocks until it came to a cave.

In the center of the cave was a squirming mass of purple fur: five baby saber-toothed poodnoobies. Each baby was nearly as big as Lunk!

Suddenly Blork realized why the big saber-tooth had brought them here. "Lunk!" he cried. "It thinks *you're* one of its babies!"

Momma Saber-tooth dropped Lunk into the pile of babies, then stood watching to make sure he didn't try to escape.

Blork tried to decide what to do next. He wanted to get down with Lunk, but he was afraid if he did, the babies might eat him. Or maybe Momma Saber-tooth would think he was a menace and want to get him away from her babies—in which case *she* might eat him just to get rid of him.

But he couldn't stay clinging to her back forever.

The saber-tooth solved the question for him. As if suddenly noticing he was there, she gave herself another great shake.

Blork's grip slipped and he went flying against the wall.

"OW!" he shouted as he bounced down among the babies.

They looked almost exactly like Lunk, except their faces were still baby sweet, and they had enormous fangs curving down from the front of their mouths.

When Lunk saw Blork he began to lick him. He used his middle tongue (poodnoobies have three), which was the medium rough one.

The pood-puppies began to lick him, too.

It was cute, but disgusting.

Soon Blork was soggy with poodnoobie slobber.

"Cut it out, you guys!" he cried.

When they didn't stop, he started trying to push himself away from them. Momma Sabertooth saw this and made a warning snort. With a sigh, Blork settled back to the floor of the nest. The pood-puppies snuggled around him, drooling and burping.

The pood-puppies were warm and cuddly (except for their giant teeth). They squirmed and jostled, then began to settle down. After a while they went to sleep.

After a little while longer Blork went to sleep, too.

When Blork woke up, it was dark. The moon was shining through the front of the poodnoobie's cave. In the distance he could hear a weird, mournful howl.

Suddenly he felt a hand on his shoulder.

"What—" he started to shout.

"*Shhhh,*" hissed Moomie Peevik. "I came to get you out of here."

"How did you find me?"

"Conquering Female Warrior Scouts learn all about tracking."

"Great. But I can't go without Lunk!"

"Of course not."

Blork looked around, trying to figure out which of the furry lumps was Lunk. It wasn't easy, because it was so dark. But then he noticed that the moonlight sparkled on the pood-puppies' fangs.

Finally he found a poodnoobie without fangs. "Come on, Lunkie," he whispered in its ears. "We have to go."

Lunk burped and licked his face, but didn't wake up.

"Come on!" said Blork, a little bit louder. He gave Lunk a shake.

Lunk snorted and opened his eyes. Blork wrapped his hands around Lunk's mouth. Then he leaned close to Lunk's ear and whispered, "Shhhhh! Follow me!"

With Moomie Peevik leading the way, they started out of the cave. It wasn't easy getting around the baby poodnoobies, and at first Blork was afraid he was going to wake them. But they slept as soundly as Lunk, and did nothing but snort and sputter, even if you stepped right on them.

They slipped out of the mouth of the cave. The moonlight sparkled on the swamp. Above them twinkled a billion, billion stars, their patterns unlike any Blork knew in his own time.

"It's beautiful," whispered Moomie Peevik.

"AARRRRAAAAANK!" bellowed something behind them.

"Uh-oh," said Blork.

4

YOO-HOO, WHO?

Rising from the murky water of the swamp was a clear, blobby form. It stretched higher and higher, outlined against the dark sky— which Blork could see through its transparent body. Small chunks of stuff moved and twitched within the outline.

"What is *that*?" whispered Moomie Peevik. She stepped closer to Blork.

"I don't know!" he replied. "But I don't think—"

The thing moaned and began to tilt in their direction.

"Run!" cried Moomie Peevik.

Blork agreed completely. Unfortunately, they chose different directions to do their running. After a minute Blork realized he was splashing through the swamp alone.

"Lunk!" he cried. "Moomie Peevik! Where are you?"

They did not answer. The only sounds that came to him through the prehistoric darkness were the weird and mournful cries of great, unknown beasts.

Blork turned in a slow circle, hoping he could find some sign of Lunk or Moomie Peevik. He would even have been glad to find the way back to Momma Saber-tooth's cave. But he couldn't see the tiniest clue as to which way he had come.

Cold and frightened, Blork stumbled on. He wanted to call out to his friends, but didn't dare. It seemed more likely he would attract the attention of something big and hungry instead. So he plodded along, splash—splash—splashing through the murky water. Wings whirred above him. Swamp gas bubbled and popped out of the water, stinking worse than a fremmis burp. Weird cries echoed in the distance.

Suddenly Blork saw a soft light ahead of him. His first thought was to run toward it. Then he remembered that there shouldn't *be* a light in this swamp, and slowed down again.

Walking more carefully, trying not to splash anymore, Blork continued toward the light. It came from a clump of tall, thick plants. When Blork reached the plants, he stood behind one and peered around the edge.

He blinked in surprise. The light was coming from a small person. He had huge ears, a wrinkled face with kind eyes, and a curling tail. He was sitting in the middle of a big blossom. Raising one hand, he gestured for Blork to step forward.

"Who are you?" asked Blork, staying right where he was.

"Yoo-hoo."

"What?"

"Yoo-hoo!"

"I'm Blork," said Blork, trying not to lose his temper. "Who you?"

"I told you twice, my name is Yoo-hoo!"

"Yoo-hoo?"

"Yes? Did you want something?"

"I want to get out of here!"

"But you just got here."

"I mean out of this swamp. Out of this time, for that matter." He paused and looked at the little man suspiciously. "What are you doing here, anyway?"

"I'm not."

"Not what?"

"I'm not here," said the little man, spreading his arms and smiling.

Blork rolled his eyes. "What are you talking about?"

"What you see is merely my image. I came back to find you because my friend Old BeBop Kenoobie, whom you met on the Planet of the Dips, asked me to keep an eye out for you."

He reached up to his face, pulled out one of his eyes, and held it out to Blork. "Here you go!"

"Yuck!" cried Blork.

"Sorry," said Yoo-hoo, popping his eye back into its socket. "Old joke. Used to work better than it does now. Anyway, Kenoobie was worried about what might happen to you after you left the Planet of the Dips, so he asked me to keep track of you. I must say that flinging yourself several million years into the past was even worse than he expected."

"We didn't do it on purpose."

"People usually don't," said Yoo-hoo with a sigh. "Anyway, I'm actually home in my bathtub. As I said, this is just an image of me."

"No offense, but what good does that do me?" asked Blork. Something slithered over his foot, and he stepped forward to get away from it.

"Well, I can't wrestle monsters for you in this form. But I can give you fabulously good advice. After all, I am an incredibly wise and ancient person—not to mention the master of seventeen mental arts, a warrior of galactic renown, and a terribly cute little fellow."

"So what's your advice?"

Yoo-hoo put a stubby finger beside his wide flat nose, scrunched up his face so that his eyes nearly disappeared among the wrinkles, then whispered, "You must see with your heart."

And with that, he faded out of sight.

"That was about as useful as buttons on a rock," muttered Blork.

Suddenly Yoo-hoo returned. "By the way, I forgot to mention: You must be careful not to change the past. Move one little rock and you may destroy the future as you know it. On the other hand, it may be that you actually are part of the past, and have already done everything you are here to do, so if you don't do it, the future you know won't exist. I can never remember which way it is. Never mind. I get confused. Sorry I am. Later will you see I. Bye-bye! Don't kiss any wooden farfnarks!"

With that, he faded out of sight again, leaving Blork more confused than ever. But as Blork turned to leave the clearing, Yoo-hoo appeared again. "I just remembered the rule! You have to leave everything here. If you try to take anything out of the past, *that's* what will mess things up! It could totally destroy the future."

"Got it," said Blork. "Thanks."

"My pleasure," said Yoo-hoo's voice. The image itself had already vanished.

Blork stood still, expecting Yoo-hoo to show up yet one more time. After several minutes went by without the little man appearing, Blork left the clearing. As he squished through the swamp, he thought about the things Yoo-hoo had said.

What the heck was "See with your heart" supposed to mean?

He closed his eyes and tried it.

All that happened was that he ran into a plant and fell down.

As he was trying to get back out of the muck, he heard a sound behind him. It was Momma Saber-tooth. She didn't look happy.

Blork screamed and tried to run. He wasn't fast enough. Momma Saber-tooth snatched him up in her great jaws. She gave him a little shake—not rough, just enough so he could feel it—then trotted back the way she had come.

Blork squirmed and struggled. He shouted and screamed. He banged on her fangs with his fists.

She wouldn't let go until she got back to the cave. Then she dropped him into the pile of pood-puppies and went to lay down in front of the door.

To Blork's relief, Lunk was in the pile as well. "Boy, am I glad to see you," said Blork, throwing his arms around Lunk's neck.

Lunk licked him with all three tongues at once.

The giant pood-puppies snuggled around them.

Blork looked at the entrance. As near as he could tell, Momma Saber-tooth had adopted him along with Lunk. She considered them her babies, and she wasn't about to let them run loose. But what about the others? Had Moomie Peevik gotten lost in the swamp, or had she made her way back to the ship? Was Dr. Pimento trying to fix things—and if so, was he making them better, or worse? Skippy was probably getting crankier by the moment. And Appus Meko might have turned into a quivering mass of terrified jelly by this point.

They were his crew.

He was their captain.

He had to get back and help them!

He stood up, ready to charge the door.

Before he could move, something thick and gooey wrapped around his neck.

5

TOO MUCH GOO

Yarrrgh!" cried Blork. "Yeeagh ack murfle—"

Then he made no more sounds, because the gooey thing had covered his mouth as well.

It began pulling him toward the back of the cave. Blork struggled and squirmed. He thrashed and squiggled. He grabbed at the floor, but found nothing to hold except loose rocks.

Momma Saber-tooth heard the commotion and came bounding across the floor toward him. It was too late. Blork had been pulled through a crack in the back of the cave.

Now he was in complete darkness, a darkness deeper than any he had ever known.

And still the slimy, gooey thing pulled him on.

Soon Blork felt himself being dragged into water. "Hey!" he shouted, struggling harder than ever.

The gooeyness oozed over his head, completely surrounding it.

This is the end, Blork thought. But to his surprise, he found his face was inside an air bubble. He could breathe!

As Blork was pulled through the cold, dark water, squiggly things brushed against him. He couldn't see them, but in his imagination they were huge and horrible. He was terrified one of them might decide he would make a tasty snack.

After a long time he was pulled back out of the water. The gooey stuff slid away from him. Blork was sitting in mud. Oozy, squishy mud. He was in a cave. He could tell it was a cave because the walls were coated with glowing fungus. The light was soft and green, a little like the eyes of the robot that had taken care of Blork when he was little.

Though he wanted to shout, Blork didn't make a sound. He didn't want to attract the attention of whatever had dragged him here. He counted to a hundred, and then to a hundred again. Then he couldn't stand it anymore, and he did shout.

Actually, he bellowed.

"WHAT THE HECK IS GOING ON HERE?"

The goo wrapped around his head again.

He could feel it oozing into his ears.

"Hey, cut that—*mmmmrphle ACK!*"

Now the goo was in his mouth, and his nose, too.

And then, suddenly, not only did he have goo in his mouth and his ears and his nose, he had pictures in his mind.

The thing that had grabbed him was telling him a story.

The story started in the water. Blork saw a little creature, a single cell, oozing around, eating whatever it could find.

He had seen things like this in science class. He figured soon the creature would split in half and become two creatures.

But it didn't. It just kept eating, and growing.

And growing.

And growing.

After a while the creature was the size of his fist.

Then it was the size of his head.

In the swampy waters around it, life changed and developed. The clear cell kept eating things, only now they were bigger things, things that swam and squiggled. More time rolled past. *Lots* of time. Hundreds of years. Thousands of years. Millions and millions of years.

The creature grew more slowly now, but it didn't stop. It was like a giant water balloon, getting more and more full. Except what was

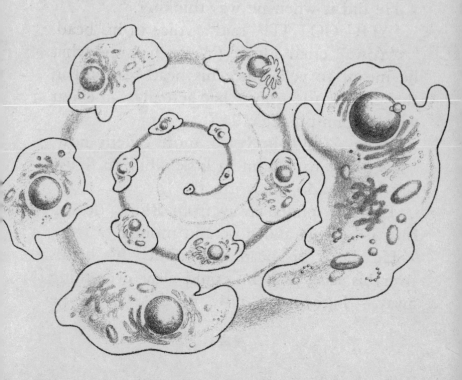

inside wasn't really water, it was—well, creature stuff.

Then came a picture Blork couldn't understand at first.

The creature stretched out a chunk of itself, and began tapping it against the rest of itself.

What was that supposed to mean?

Blork thought about it. Where had he seen that gesture before? Then he remembered. Dr. Pimento made it all the time (only he was tapping his head, not just a blob).

He did it when he was thinking.

"YOU GOT IT!" said a voice in his head.

"Yow!" cried Blork. (Well, that was what he meant to yell. Since his head was still in the grip of the goo, what actually came out was "Mmmrph-grgle!")

"Sorry," said the voice, more quietly now. "It's going to take me a little while to figure out how to do this correctly."

The goo pulled away from Blork, oozing out of his ears and nose and mouth.

He shook his head and rubbed his hands over his face, as if he could clear everything away. "Figure out how to do what?" he asked. He was feeling very cranky. But he tried not to sound too nasty. He didn't want to get re-gooed.

"How to talk to you. Oh, this is wonderful! I didn't know there was such a thing as talking until I got hold of your brain. Oh, lovely, lovely, lovely! This is much easier than trying to send you all those pictures. Pictures are good. They worked for the first part of the story. But it's hard to send a picture of thinking."

"So that was you in the story?" asked Blork.

"Well, of course it was me. Why would I tell you someone else's story? Anyway, I got right to the part where I started to think. It was amazing. I'd been drifting around in the swamp for millions of years, and all of a sudden one day I just realized I was alive. I mean, I had never thought about it before. Well, I'd never thought anything before. But do you know what an amazing thing it is to realize you exist?"

"I hadn't really thought about it," said Blork.

"You ought to. It's astonishing." The creature was silent for a moment. "Anyway, there

I was, filled with the thought that I existed, and I had no one to tell it to. I was not only the biggest thing in the swamp, and the smartest, I was the loneliest. *Lonely*. That's a good word. I'm glad I found it in your brain."

"What were you doing in my brain any-way?" asked Blork. He put his hands to his head, as if to be sure it was still all there.

"Trying to find out what was in there. But

I never expected to find anything as wonderful as this."

"As what?"

"Talking."

Blork was confused. "How could you learn it so fast?"

"I'm smart. Very smart. Very, *very* smart, actually. You have to remember, I've been floating around for millions of years. Also, language is my best subject. I'm not very good at math. That's why I never learned to divide."

"So why did you bring me here?"

"I told you, I'm lonely. When I saw you and your friend . . ." The creature stopped for a moment. *"Friend.* What a good word! Delicious, really. Anyway, when I saw you and your friend come out of the cave, I was curious—and very upset when you ran away. I was still floating there, feeling sad, when Momma Saber-tooth brought you back. So I oozed into the cave through an underground stream. I wanted to find out what you were all about. I had no idea you were going to be so interesting!"

"I'm glad," said Blork. "Now, do you suppose you could take me back to the others?"

"Why should I take you back? I've been waiting for someone like you for millions of years. You're mine. I found you, and I'm going to keep you."

6

HEART, BROKEN

Blork almost had a tantrum. He stopped himself at the very last second. If he made this thing mad, it might just swallow him— or whatever you called it when a blob like this stuffed you inside itself to eat you.

It was a close call. The tantrum *wanted* to come out. Blork quivered and quaked. He trembled and vibrated. His eyes bulged. Little snorts came out his nose holes.

"What are you doing?" asked the blob.

"Holding in a tantrum!" shouted Blork.

"Oh, a tantrum. I learned that word inside your head. But a tantrum is something you do when you're mad. Why are you mad?"

"Why am I mad?" roared Blork, finding it harder to keep his temper when he was being asked a stupid question. "I'm mad because you won't let me go back where I belong!"

"What difference does it make? You had friends back there. You have a friend here. Me. Isn't one as good as the other?"

Blork looked at the blob in astonishment. "You don't get it, do you?"

"Probably not. I'm very bright, but I'm not very good socially."

"Well, you haven't had much chance to practice," said Blork. He felt some sympathy, since he was not very good socially himself. "Of course," he added slyly, "if you took me back to the ship, you could practice with all of us."

"Could I really?" cried the blob. "That would be . . . what's that word I found in your head? Oh, I know. That would be cool!"

"Great!" said Blork. "Let's go."

"Not right away. I have to rest first. Besides, I want to get to know you a little better before I do. But I will take you back. I promise."

And with that the blob oozed back down into the water. It blended in so well that Blork couldn't tell if it was even there anymore.

He sighed and settled down to wait, which was about his least favorite thing in the world.

Alone in the cave, he didn't have much to do except worry and think. Worrying didn't do him any good. So he decided to think.

He thought about his adventures.

He thought about his tantrums.

He thought about his crew. Then thinking and worrying sort of got mushed together. Had Moomie Peevik gotten back safely? Where was Lunk? What was happening to the crew? Did they miss him? Were they worried about him?

Would they leave without him if they got the ship fixed before he got back?

Would they *ever* get the ship fixed?

"This is stupid," said Blork, standing up. "I'm not going to solve anything this way." He started to explore the cave, looking for a way out.

He had not gone more than a few feet when a piece of the blob reached out of the water, wrapped itself around his leg, and pulled him back. "You weren't going to leave me, were you?" it asked mournfully.

Blork was about to reply that yes, he certainly was going to leave, when he saw something so strange he almost swallowed his tongue. In the center of the great blob he saw the glowing figure of Yoo-hoo. Holding up one stubby finger, the strange old person whispered, "Remember, Blork: You must learn to see with your heart."

Blork snorted. "Yeah, right."

"I don't under- stand the answer," said the blob.

Blork shook his head and blinked. Had he been dreaming?

He looked at the blob again. It was quivering. When Blork quivered it usually meant he was angry. But the blob didn't sound angry. Could it be something else?

Blork closed his eyes. He tried to see with his heart.

At first, nothing happened. Then, perhaps because he had already been connected to the blob, he saw it in front of him; saw it even though his eyes were still closed.

And what he saw was the loneliest creature on the planet Splat. The loneliness seemed to surround the blob like a dark cloud.

Of course it's lonely, thought Blork. *It's*

never, ever had anyone to talk to. He sighed. "No, I wasn't going to leave you."

"Good! Now, what shall we do? Wait, I know—let's play a game!"

"How do you know about games?"

"I found them in your head."

It wasn't easy to figure out what to play with the blob. Hide-and-seek didn't work. When Blork tried to look for the blob, it always hid in the water—which wasn't really fair, since it blended in so perfectly he could never see it. And when Blork tried to hide, the blob somehow always knew where he was. It claimed it was because it could sense his heart.

Blork made a face. "Don't be mushy," he said.

They couldn't play ball, because they didn't have one.

And they couldn't play Splatoonian Squish-Bonk, because they didn't have enough players. Or bonksticks, for that matter.

Tag was the best game, mostly because the fun was to see how far the blob could stretch a piece of itself to touch Blork.

On the third day the blob said, "This has been fun. Now I will take you back. I want to meet your other friends."

It wrapped Blork in a bubble inside itself. Then it went back underwater.

Sometimes as they traveled the blob would wrap itself around some other creature. It kept these in bubbles apart from the one where it had Blork. Slowly they would disappear. Finally Blork realized the blob was eating them.

Twice the blob went to the surface to put fresh air in Blork's bubble.

Finally they returned to the top of the swamp. The blob lurched onto dry land. It spit out Blork.

"Your ship is that way," it said, pointing a piece of itself. "I'll follow you."

Blork took about ten steps. Suddenly he heard a snap.

Something grabbed his foot.

He felt a rush of air as he was yanked upward.

7

TOGETHER, AGAIN

When Blork opened his eyes again, the ground was a long way below him. He looked up and saw a vine wrapped around his right foot. The vine was tied to a treetop.

"What's going on here?" he roared.

No one answered. But a moment later something came crashing through the bushes. Blork started to shout again, then stopped, so astonished that he didn't know what to say.

Moomie Peevik, dressed in fur and carrying a spear, was riding Momma Saber-tooth.

"Blork!" she cried in surprise. "You're alive!"

"Of course I'm alive. Get me down from here!"

Moomie Peevik steered Momma Saber-tooth so that the big creature was standing right under Blork. Then she stretched up and used the edge of her spear to cut the rope that held him.

Blork plopped onto Momma Saber-tooth's back. He started to slide off, but Moomie Peevik grabbed him and pulled him back. He got a fistful of fur, and managed to drag himself into a sitting position.

Once he was sure he wasn't going to fall off he looked at Moomie Peevik more carefully. "You look like a wild woman," he said at last.

Moomie Peevik threw back her head and laughed. "I *am* a wild woman. As long as we're lost in a prehistoric jungle, I figured I might as well work on my Conquering

Female Warrior Scout Wild Woman merit badge. That's why I built this trap."

"Well, you should definitely get your badge," said Blork. "The trap works fine. Now let's go back to the ship."

"I don't know," said Moomie Peevik, looking at him carefully. "We're supposed to eat what we catch."

"Moomie!"

She sighed. "Oh, I suppose I can skip it this time."

"Where did you get that outfit, anyway?" asked Blork.

"I had the ship make it. We've got some of the stuff working again." She turned around. "Do you like it?"

"It's a little scary."

Moomie Peevik scowled at him. Then she plunked herself down on Momma Sabertooth's neck. "Come on, girl," she said. "Let's get going."

"How did you tame her?" asked Blork.

"Never mind. You might think it was a little scary. Besides, it's a Conquering Female Warrior Scout secret."

Suddenly the blob, which had been waiting under a tree, made a slight burbling noise.

Moomie Peevik turned toward it, then gasped. Lowering the point of her spear, she pointed it right at the blob. "What is *that?*" she asked through clenched teeth.

"It's . . . a friend," said Blork, feeling a little uneasy. "It—" He turned to the blob and whispered, "You are an it, aren't you?"

"Definitely!"

"It wanted to meet the rest of us," said Blork.

Moomie Peevik scowled. "I suppose it can come with us," she said. Then, speaking directly to the blob, she added: "But no funny business. This spear is loaded, and I know how to use it!"

Blork and the blob followed Moomie Peevik and Momma Saber-tooth back to the ship.

Lunk and the pood-puppies were lolling about in the shade underneath it. They were burping and drooling, and looked quite happy. Blabber was running around them, trying to get one of them to chase him. Blork was relieved to see that Lunk was all right. He just hoped his pet wasn't going to turn into a wild thing, too.

The rest of the crew was also there. Skippy was sitting on the ground, looking truly, deeply grumpy. He had his propeller hat in front of him, and was pulling wires out of it. Appus Meko was standing on top of the ship, his back to them, staring into the distance. Dr. Pimento stood at the edge of the clearing. He had arranged some stones in a row and was hitting them with a pair of hammers. He kept bending over to listen to them.

"What's the doc doing?" asked Blork.

Moomie Peevik shrugged. "He says he's trying to invent rock music. So far it just sounds like a lot of noise."

"And why is Skippy looking so cranky?"

"I'll tell you why Skippy is cranky!" shouted Skippy, whose hearing was better than Blork expected.

"He's cranky because he has to *roll* anywhere he wants to go."

With that, he flung himself sideways and rolled over to where Blork and Moomie Peevik were standing. "My solar perplexus ran out," he growled, staring up at Blork. "And now my propeller won't work!"

The look on his face was truly tragic. He stared at Blork for a moment, then added, "Oh, by the way, I'm glad you're alive. Where have you been?"

"With me," burbled the blob, rearing up behind him.

"Yike!" cried Skippy, rolling away as fast as he could.

Dr. Pimento looked up from his rocks. Appus Meko spun around. "Blork!" they cried. "You're back! We were afraid you had been swallowed by something."

"He was," said the blob proudly.

Because you could see right through the blob, it was easy to miss until it called attention to itself. Now Appus Meko did see it. "Yikes!" he cried. "We're all gonna—"

"Oh, skip it!" shouted everyone.

Dr. Pimento hurried over to Blork and the blob. "Nice to see you," he said, patting Blork on the head. Then he dropped to his knees and started examining the blob.

"Fascinating," he muttered, taking out his pocket computer and scribbling a note.

The blob oozed forward and swallowed him.

Everyone started to shout and scream.

"Wait, wait," said Blork. "I think it will be all right."

A moment later the blob spit Dr. Pimento out. It burped, then said, "Fascinating. Also, brilliant. But weird. *Very* weird."

"We already knew that," snorted Skippy.

"Anyway," continued the blob, "now that I have had a chance to absorb what's in Dr. Pimento's brain, I know what's wrong with your ship. I also know where to find the things you need."

"Fascinating!" cried Skippy.

"What the heck is going on here!" said Moomie Peevik.

"If everyone will calm down, I'll explain," said Blork.

They calmed down.

He explained.

When he was done, the blob added, "I am very pleased to meet all of you. I hope we will be good friends."

"Okay, just as long as you don't swallow me," said Appus Meko.

"This is going to be a beautiful partnership!" said Dr. Pimento, clasping his hands in delight.

"Kreegah, kreegah bundolo!" said Moomie Peevik.

Blork looked at her.

"Just practicing," she said. Then she went off to polish her spear.

That night Blork had a dream. In the dream he was trying to crack a nut. When he finally did get it open, Yoo-hoo popped out of the shell. He pulled out one of his eyeballs and tossed it over his shoulder. "You must see with your *heart*," he whispered.

Then he faded away.

Blork tossed and turned, trying to see with his heart.

All that happened was that he got a stomachache.

As the days went by, the crew fell into a pattern.

Moomie Peevik would go out and hunt for food.

Dr. Pimento and the blob would figure out what was the next thing to be done on the ship.

Then Blork, Appus Meko, and Skippy would go out to gather what they needed. Sometimes this meant long trips to places the blob told them about. (Skippy didn't start going along until they had found what they needed to fix his solar perplexus.)

In the evening they would sit around a campfire and talk. Sometimes Skippy would tell stories. Moomie Peevik taught them songs from the Conquering Female Warrior Scouts, including "I Gave My Love a Planet" and "If It Moves, Blast It!" When it was time to go to bed, the blob would squirt a little goo on the fire and put it out. Then it would ooze its way back to the swamp, because it couldn't stay out of the water too long.

Finally the day came when they were ready to try the ship.

The crew gathered their things.

Momma Saber-tooth and the pood-puppies watched them. They looked puzzled, and worried.

Just as the crew was about to climb the ramp into the ship, the blob cried, "I can't let you go!"

"But you have to," said Blork.

"I can't!" sobbed the blob. "I'll be too lonely!"

Then it reared up and swallowed them.

8

DIVIDE AND CONQUER

The crew was trapped in a giant bubble inside the blob.

"We're all gonna die!" cried Appus Meko.

"Actually, we're more likely to be *digested*," pointed out Dr. Pimento, poking at the edge of the bubble.

"Can't you say anything useful, you silly stick?" growled Skippy.

"Luddle-luddle-luddle," babbled Blabber.

Moomie Peevik picked him up. He hid his face against her furry outfit.

Blork could tell from his friends' eyes that they were terrified. He was scared, too, but not as scared as the rest of them, since he had already been inside the blob.

What he was mostly was furious.

"Blob!" he cried. "Blob, you let us out!"

"I can't," said the blob sadly. "If I do, you'll go away. Then I will be alone. I don't want to be alone again. I have to keep you here."

"But you knew we were going to leave when you helped us fix the ship," said Blork, feeling confused.

"I was being friendly. I was being helpful. And it made you like me. But I didn't *truly* understand what I was doing until today. Then I saw you start to leave, and I knew I couldn't let it happen."

"But what are you going to do with us?" asked Blork. "You can't keep us inside you forever."

"Actually, I think I can."

"I've got an idea!" whispered Moomie Peevik. "Let's ask the blob if it wants to come back to the future with us."

"Oh, brilliant," said Skippy. "Then any time it doesn't like what one of us is doing, it can swallow us again."

Moomie Peevik tightened her grip on her spear. "You got a better idea, buster?" she asked grimly.

"I think it's a very good idea," said Dr. Pimento. "I like the blob."

"I like it, too," said Blork. "At least, I did until just now. Maybe we could—"

He had been about to agree that perhaps they could bring the blob along. But suddenly he remembered Yoo-hoo's warning: *You have to leave everything here. If you try to take any-thing out of the past,* that's *what will mess things up! It could totally destroy the future.*

"We can't do it," he said.

"Why not?" asked Moomie Peevik.

Blork told her what Yoo-hoo had said.

"Then what are we going to do?" whined Appus Meko.

Blork thought about it some more. He thought about everything that had happened. He thought about his friends and how much he cared about them. He thought about the other thing Yoo-hoo had said:

You must learn to see with your heart.

He didn't know what good that would do. But if Yoo-hoo was as wise as he claimed to be, it must mean something.

Blork remembered that he had managed to see with his heart the first time he was inside the blob.

Maybe he could do it again now.

He looked at Moomie Peevik. As long as he had his eyes open, all he could see was her face. He closed his eyes. He tried to keep seeing her, just the way he had once seen the blob. After a little while he felt a warm glow inside him, a glow filled with strength and kindness.

"What are you doing?" said Appus Meko.

"Shhhh!" said Blork, holding up one hand.

He turned toward Dr. Pimento. His heart saw a blaze of light that kept twisting and fading, then shining brighter than ever. Curious, friendly, kind, and dippy.

He turned toward Appus Meko and saw loneliness, which surprised him, until he thought about it. He looked harder. Then he saw something that astonished him. It was admiration.

He looked at Skippy and saw a toasted skiffle. It took him a minute to realize that this meant the pudgy Dip was hard and crusty on the outside, but warm and soft on the inside.

He looked at Lunk and saw simple love. Well, love and hunger.

And in every single one of them he saw one more thing: They were counting on *him* to solve this problem. He was their captain, and he was the one who had to get them out of this mess.

And at last he knew what he had to do.

"Blob," he said. "Oh, Blobbie. I'll tell you what. If you let the others go, I will stay here with you."

"You can't do that!" cried Moomie Peevik.

"I can if I have to."

"It's a deal!" said the blob quickly. Then *Phut! Phut! Phut!* it spit out the crew—everyone except Blork.

Blork looked out at the world through the clear side of the blob.

He could see his crew looking in at him.

And then he saw something else, something totally unexpected.

He saw Moomie Peevik begin to tremble.

The tremble grew to a shake.

Her eyes got wide. Smoke started coming out her ears.

She was going to have a tantrum!

"I can't believe it!" she cried, vaulting onto Momma Saber-tooth's back. "I can't believe you're such a greedy, selfish . . . *blob!*"

And then the tantrum erupted.

But this was no mere tantrum. It was a Genuine World-Class Conquering Female Warrior Scout Wild Woman Tantrum.

Great howls of rage pierced the prehistoric skies.

Strange and ancient beasts answered across the distance.

Giant mushrooms toppled.

Feathery leaves curled up and fell off the weird trees.

Moomie Peevik raged and ranted. She broke her spear in half and twirled both parts around her head until the air hummed. She flung herself at the blob, screaming, "YOU GREAT BIG UCKY PIECE OF PROTOPLASM! YOU LET MY FRIEND GO!"

The blob began to quiver. It began to quake.

"YEAGGA ARGLE BARGLE BARGLE!" screamed Moomie Peevik, jumping up and down.

The blob spit out Blork.

He landed at Moomie Peevik's feet. Her eyes were wild and her breast was heaving.

Blabber was hiding underneath Lunk, going "Uh-oh, uh-oh, uh-oh."

"Wow!" said Blork. "That was great!"

Moomie Peevik took a deep breath. She began to smile. "I learned from a master," she said.

The blob heaved a great sigh.

"My heart is breaking!" it sobbed.

Suddenly it began to tremble.

"Good grief!" cried Dr. Pimento. *"Mitosis!"*

"Your toes is what?" asked Skippy.

"Not me, the blob! It's . . . it's . . ."

"It's splitting," said Blork in awe.

9

HOME AT LAST

Everyone stared at the blob. Its middle was pinching in.

The pinching got tighter and tighter.

As it did, the blob bulged out at both ends.

And then it happened. The blob split in half.

"You did it!" cried Blork. "You learned to divide."

"I could feel myself being torn in two," said both halves of the blob, speaking at the same time.

"Part of my heart wants to keep you here," said the blob on the right.

"The other part knows I have to let you go," said the blob on the left.

"You don't have a heart," pointed out Appus Meko.

"Don't be a doofus," said Skippy. "The blob—er, *blobs*—just mean that whatever part of them feels emotion was in bad shape."

"But this is perfect!" cried Blork.

"It is?" asked everyone.

"Of course," said Blork. "Now the blob has what it always wanted: company!"

"Wow!" cried both halves of the blob. Rearing up, they threw glops of themselves around each other in a big, blobby hug.

"Careful!" warned Dr. Pimento. "You don't want to end up squishing yourself back together."

"I've never been so happy," said half the blob.

"Neither have I," said th

"Thank you, thank yo

both halves, reaching out to pat Blork and
Moomie Peevik on their heads.

The crew decided to spend one more night
in the past. They had a big party, with a bon-
fire and lots of good food, including special
treats for Lunk, Blabber, and Momma Saber-
tooth and her babies. (Now that the ship was
working again, the food-i-lators could make
anything they wanted.)

Moomie Peevik had the ship make Wild
People outfits for everyone. Then she led the

crew in a wild dance. They stomped and shouted, and their cries of joy rang through the skies of ancient Splat.

The blobs sat on opposite sides of the campfire, watching. They kept waving to each other.

Late that night, when the campfire was dying down, the blobs said good-bye to everyone.

"We do not want to be here in the morning to watch you go," they said.

"We're glad for you," said the blob on the left.

"But it will be too sad for us," said the blob on the right.

Then they oozed off into the swamp and disappeared.

The next morning the crew got ready to leave ancient Splat.

Appus Meko went back into the closet that would direct the Whoopee Warp where to take them.

To Blork's surprise, he did it without complaining.

"Just don't let that fuzzygrumper in with me," said Appus Meko as he was about to close the door.

"I'll hold him myself," promised Moomie Peevik, who had changed back into her uniform.

The takeoff was perfect. The ship roared into space.

Dr. Pimento crossed the special wires.

They were flung into the Whoopee Warp. When Skippy knocked Dr. Pimento's hands apart, they found themselves still hovering right above Splat.

They were in the very same place they had been.

Even so, the planet beneath them looked different.

Millions of years different.

"Home at last!" cried Blork.

"It's been a long, strange trip," said Moomie Peevik.

"You're not kidding," said Appus Meko. "Since Squat first kidnapped us, we've been to the Planet of Cranky People, the Planet of the Dips, and the swamps of Prehistoric Splat."

"The only place we haven't been is the Galactic Celebration," said Blork a little sadly.

The Galactic Celebration was supposed to have been the biggest party in the history of the galaxy. Blork had been invited to get a medal for saving the city from his evil twin. But by now the big party was long over.

When they landed the ship in front of the Block 78 Child House, all the kids came streaming out to see what was going on.

The Childkeeper rolled in circles. "Oh,

mercy me, mercy me, mercy me," it moaned, clutching its metallic hands together.

"Lower the ramp, Officer Moomie," said Blork.

"Aye-aye, Captain Blork!"

A moment later Blork, Moomie Peevik, and Appus Meko appeared at the top of the ramp.

A great cheer went up.

"Great Sputtering Star Systems!" said Blork. "Look at that!"

Standing on the lawn in front of the Child House was a statue of Blork, Moomie Peevik, and Appus Meko! The Blork part had a shiny medal hanging around its neck.

"When you didn't show up for so long, everyone thought you were dead!" explained the Childkeeper. "We raised this statue in your honor."

"We weren't dead," said Blork. "Just misplaced."

Murgo and Lakka climbed up the statue and lifted the medal over its head. They brought it to the real Blork and hung it around his neck.

"Everyone in the galaxy has been wondering what happened to you three," said the Childkeeper.

"We've been making new friends," said Blork. "And here come two of them," he added as Skippy and Dr. Pimento appeared at the door of the ship.

"Uh-oh," said the Childkeeper. "Better go make some more dinner!"

Muttering to itself, it rolled back into the Child House.

Three nights later Blork and his friends met back in the ship.

Blork took the medal from around his neck. He hung it on the ship's wall.

"This is not mine," he said. "It is ours. We're a team, and whatever we do, we do together."

"And what shall we do now?" asked Moo-mie Peevik. A Wild Woman twinkle sparkled in her eyes.

"I don't know," said Blork. "It's nice here, and I was glad to see our friends. But I think—"

"It's time for an adventure!" cried Appus Meko.

"Aren't you afraid we're going to die?" sneered Skippy.

Appus Meko shrugged. "Of course. But if

we just hang around and do nothing, I'll die anyway, sooner or later."

"Are we all agreed?" asked Blork.

One by one the crew nodded their heads.

Blork looked at Moomie Peevik.

"Blast off!" he said.

"Aye-aye, Captain!"

She pushed the zoomstick.

The rockets roared.

Blork and his crew headed for the stars.

About the Author and the Illustrator

BRUCE COVILLE was born in Syracuse, New York. He grew up in a rural area north of the city, around the corner from his grandparents' dairy farm. In the years before he was able to make his living full-time as a writer, Bruce was, among other things, a gravedigger, a toymaker, a magazine editor, and a door-to-door salesman. He loves reading, musical theater, and being outdoors.

In addition to more than sixty books for young readers, Bruce has written poems, plays, short stories, newspaper articles, thousands of letters, and several years' worth of journal entries.

Some of Bruce's best-known books are *My Teacher Is an Alien*, *Goblins in the Castle*, and *Aliens Ate My Homework*.

KATHERINE COVILLE is a self-taught artist who is known for her ability to combine finely detailed drawings with a deliciously wacky sense of humor. She is also a toymaker, specializing in creatures hitherto unseen on this planet. Her other collaborations with Bruce Coville include *The Monster's Ring*, *The Foolish Giant*, *Sarah's Unicorn*, *Goblins in the Castle*, *Aliens Ate My Homework*, and the *Space Brat* series.

The Covilles live in a brick house in Syracuse along with their youngest child, three cats, and a jet-powered Norwegian elkhound named Thor.